A CHILD'S CHRISTMAS in NEW ENGLAND

by ROBERT SULLIVAN
illustrated by GLENN WOLFF

Acknowledgments

The author and illustrator would like to thank Carole Kitchel Bellew, Ib Bellew, Laura Jorstad, Joe Lops, and all others at Bunker Hill Publishing for allowing them to return to Christmas one more time. Bob would also like to thank all of the folks back in Massachusetts who participated in the adventures recounted herein, and of course his wife, Lucille Rossi, and their kids—Caroline, Mary Grace, and Jack—who, it is devoutly to be hoped, are storing up warm Christmas memories of their own. Glenn would like to thank Emily Mitchell for ongoing design therapy, and Emily Bert for her amazing support and tolerance of the many wee small hours spent conjuring New England. He is also extremely grateful for the richness of Wolff family Christmases—past, present, and, surely, yet to come. God bless them, every one.

And, of course, thanks to our readers, and a sincere Merry Christmas to you all. —R.S. and G.W.

www.bunkerhillpublishing.com
by Bunker Hill Publishing Inc.
285 River Road, Piermont
New Hampshire 03779, USA

10 9 8 7 6 5 4 3 2 1

Copyright text ©2013 Robert Sullivan
Copyright illustrations ©2013 Glenn Wolff

Library of Congress Control Number: 2013934777

ISBN 978-1-59373-151-9

Printed in China

NE CHRISTMAS was quite like the others, in those years in our town well outside of Boston, our town that was much like the other towns outside of Boston. But they must not have been ordinary or unimportant—those Christmases—since, all these years later, I see something hovering in darkness as I am falling asleep in December that forces me to ask: Did it snow two feet when I was ten or ten feet when I was two, and if it is the latter case, did my parents simply tell me about it, since I could not really know it for myself? What do I remember, and what is imagined? All the Christmases roll down to visions of snow, or hoped-for snow, and to lights.

"Where did you live?" my young daughter asks.

We lived, early on, in West Chelmsford, where most of the houses, including ours, were snug against the street, which was called Main Street but saw no traffic. They were so close to the road because they had been built so very long ago, before our country was a country, and the posts for hitching horses were still standing, here and there. Behind the houses were expanses of land—in front, nothing; in back, everything—and back there we had, in warmer weather, forest, poison ivy, grapes that one year we harvested and drained in cheesecloth sacks, dripping, to make grape jelly, and, once, a bobcat. A young bobcat cried and screeched each night for a week, and its presence was news enough for the Lowell newspaper. That made us proud: our local bobcat in the *Lowell Sun*. The bobcat didn't scare me, I'm surprised to say; it excited me. It was like a nightly fireworks show—expected and fun. Human forces unknown trapped and probably killed the bobcat, no doubt working under cover of darkness. Those who were in authority did not transport and release animals back then. Suddenly, in any event, the bobcat was gone. The nights were quiet again—quiet star-filled nights.

In the West Chelmsford house, and particularly in the bedroom that Kevin and I shared, everything was angles. It was a tight house, every inch useful. We all got along—Mom, Dad, Kevin, myself—and so the compact nature of our old house was fine.

I cannot recall our main room precisely except to remember it as small and warm—warm, despite the lack of a fireplace; a hearth built in centuries past had long ago been bricked in—but I can see the tree. It was a giant tree, nearly as big as my father, who stood six feet tall. Eventually, ages six and four, my brother and I were able to assist in trimming the tree. The lights were multicolored, but most of the lights did not interest us. The bubblers did. There was liquid of some sort, probably poisonous, in their slim glass fluorescences; the fluid was warmed electrically beneath in an attached bowl, then started to bubble up. How many house fires were ignited by bubblers will never be known, and buying a bubbler today is probably as illicit an act as buying a Roman candle. But my father loved bubblers, my mother allowed them, and for Kevin and me: They were the only lights that mattered.

Except for the lights of the monastery. There was a monastery not far away—I think it was in Tyngsboro or Hudson—and the Jesuit brothers living there must have worked very hard, with huge ladders, or the church must have had much more money for maintenance than it does today, because the immense, stolid brick building was decorated to a sensational brilliance each December. We would drive through North Chelmsford in the Mercury and out onto the road by the Merrimack River, and then find the monastery, tucked away in the woods, a monastery that went ignored by all but the monks for eleven months a year. It seemed to me a magic monastery, hidden in the forest and unseeable from January to November, and then made manifest, as if by a miracle, each December. It wasn't, and then it was.

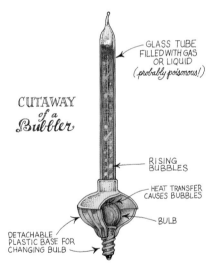

CUTAWAY *of a* Bubbler

— GLASS TUBE FILLED WITH GAS OR LIQUID (*probably poisonous!*)

— RISING BUBBLES

— HEAT TRANSFER CAUSES BUBBLES

— BULB

DETACHABLE PLASTIC BASE FOR CHANGING BULB →

My father belonged to a Catholic business group that raised money to benefit the brothers; I knew that much about the monastery. This civic association had a French name. Maybe that money helped with the lights. I knew nothing else about the relationship of brothers to fathers to nuns, and cared only about the lights—which were, again, multicolored.

M Y DAUGHTER INTERJECTS: "Our tree has white lights."

Yes, today many people prefer white lights. Your mother does. Yes, our tree has white lights. But please notice, dear: Several of them have opaque Red Sox plastic baseballs covering them and glowing gloriously with the faintest hint of red and blue. Perhaps this is my effort, perhaps this is a brushstroke of sentimentality. In my childhood years, color mattered.

We would sit in the car and look at the lights of the monastery, then would park in the dirt parking lot and, minding ice that had certainly not been sanded, proceed to the gift shop. There we would buy a present for Aunt Margot, the only person we knew who would appreciate such a thing: yet another statuette of Mary, or a Christ child in the manger, or a figurine of a Saint Nicholas–type man carrying, for some reason, a lamb, as if it were his cat. Francis of Assisi, probably.

"What else happened at Christmas?" my daughter asks.

Not too very much.

Well, I remember that one night, the phone rang. This is among my most distinct memories of West Chelmsford: the night the phone rang. The phone never rang. A week or ten days might go by without it ringing. By phone, Mom spoke only to Dad and Dad only to Mom, and even then only in emergency situations, which didn't occur except for the time that Mom left the laundry too close to the toaster and the house burned down (even then, she used the neighbor's phone, not our own).

I'll tell you about the house burning down, and then about the phone call.

Ours was a very old house, built before the Revolutionary War, and I presume it was a very dry house. It was ready for the match. The match was that toaster. Mom had put the clothes on the counter, then had gone out to chat with Mrs. Demers in the yard shared by our two houses, our ancient one and their modern one. Kevin and I were playing with Mike and Mark Demers in the sandbox that Dad and Cam Demers had built for us; it must have been summertime because we were not in school, or perhaps it was in the years before we were old enough for school—perhaps I was three or four. I remember it this way: Smoke started coming out the kitchen door and Mrs. Demers (I think her name was Theresa, and she was tall and very pretty, with honey-colored hair) said, Oh, Lucille, there's a fire. Mom made a move toward our house, then thought better of it and hurried to the Demers's house to call Dad and the fire department. We four boys watched the smoke billow. I was not the least bit afraid of fire; I didn't understand it. Suddenly it registered that Teddy was inside the house, tucked in my bed, which Mom had made that morning, as she did every morning, Teddy's little brown head sticking out from the covers. Teddy was a well-worn bear that my grandmother, Mama, had bought for me one Sunday after church at Howard Johnson's restaurant. It had been in a glass case by the cash register, and then it was mine. It was the only possession I cared about. So I went to

retrieve Teddy before the fire got worse, or whatever it was that fires did. It's not that I wasn't thinking—I was thinking actively. I was thinking of saving Teddy. Kevin, Mike and Mark didn't stop me, and Mrs. Demers must not have noticed me. I walked up one of the porch steps, then the other, and was reaching for the screen door when Mom returned from her phone calls, screamed, ran across the yard and grabbed my arm. Teddy was no more, as soon the smoke was joined by flames, which danced tauntingly from the upstairs windows. One of Chelmsford's very few fire trucks arrived on our dusty street and doused the house with water. It was all very thrilling. Dad arrived and, in his calm way, thanked everyone for his or her help. I could tell he was sad. He surely knew this would be costly.

A sufficient portion of the house had been salvaged that it could be rebuilt. Meantime, we moved into Mama's Victorian house on Mount Vernon Street in Lowell, where my mom had been a girl. There was a piano in the parlor and many stairs. Lowell seemed darker than Chelmsford, but I think that was because of the large, dark house, where only yesterday two old women—Mama and Aunt Margot—had lived by themselves, and where now two old women and a young family of four lived. Kevin and I delighted in the circumstance. We prowled every nook of that house, from the coal burner in the basement to the mysteries of the attic. Up there, one afternoon, we opened an old box and found a stash of hand grenades. My grandfather, Papa, had been a lieutenant in World War I and had taught hand-grenade-throwing techniques. These were, apparently, souvenirs of his service. When Kevin and I joyfully brought down a couple of grenades to play with in Mama's small, enclosed backyard, Mama was horrified. Where did you get those, she screamed. This all led to a second visit by a fire department—the Lowell one—and they seized the box of grenades. I'm sure the weaponry had already been defused and there was nothing really to worry about. Probably.

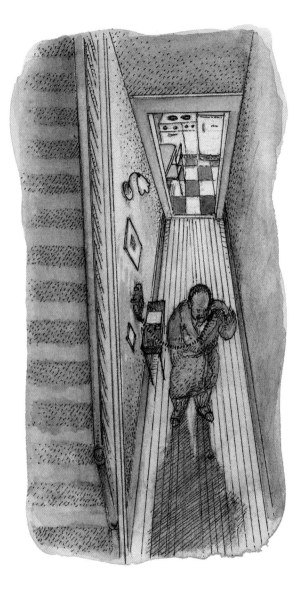

T HE STORY ABOUT THE GRENADES reminds me of the phone call. That, too, was about war.

As I said, the phone never rang. But this one night in Christmas season, the phone rang. Kevin and I were not quite asleep in our small bedroom with the peaked ceiling, and we both listened intently. Mom answered the phone, and said: "Artie, someone's calling you." Years later my brother and I pieced this episode together, at least to the extent that we needed to know it. Dad had been a master sergeant and platoon leader in World War II, and on this December evening, with the holiday drawing close, one of his men, who lived in Texas, of all places, felt the need to talk with Sergeant Sullivan. This man had figured out how to place a long-distance call to a phone on the wall by the bottom of the stairs in an old, rebuilt house in West Chelmsford, Massachusetts. Remarkable.

And why? Well, we understand much today that was incomprehensible at the time—need, fragility, perhaps mental illness—but that night all I knew: The phone rang, and that was a disturbing thing. A phone call scared me in a way that bobcats, fire and hand grenades did not.

"Really?" my daughter asks reasonably.

Yes. I'm not sure why. I think because it was so odd, but also because it was so unsettling to my father. The next morning, buttering his toast, he would not discuss it, and my mother told Kevin and me to stop asking. My dad was used to everything being normal. Even fires could be normal—an accident, after all. This wasn't normal, and I'm sure he felt there wasn't very much he could do to make the situation, whatever the situation was, any better. He talked to the fellow for a good while, and that was that.

Dad would never talk about the bad things he might have seen in the war, and he must have seen some bad things because his platoon was involved in the liberation of the horrible concentration camp at Dachau. He would only tell the humorous stories, about playing cards on the ship, about getting his men lost during the confusing Battle of the Bulge, about the warm beer in London on the way back home. If we asked him for the bad stuff, he would say, "Oh, you don't want to be bothered with that." This was okay with us. I knew we could read about that in books, and know that our father had been involved. We could put two plus two together. If he didn't want to talk about it, there was no sense in troubling him.

THER THAN THE ONE PHONE CALL and the one bobcat, the nights were very, very quiet in those years. Imagining the wind in the trees to be the sounds of reindeer on the roof still allowed, and perhaps even encouraged, a young boy to sleep soundly.

I heard those reindeer on the roof, and I think I heard Santa down the stairs, doing his best with the Erector Set, a metallic contraption that would be more Kevin's fancy than mine, and that was said to be easy to assemble— easy for Leonardo. It sounded like Santa was having trouble with it, as much trouble as he had had with the Lionel train set the year previous. I now know that a terrible, terrible phrase for Santa to encounter as his deadline nears—say, at ten thirty p.m. on Christmas Eve—is SOME ASSEMBLY REQUIRED. Dad and Mom would appear tired on Christmas morning, but very happy, and, as I look back at their faces, I see them not only happy but happy with a curious and certainly undue sense of accomplishment. Santa had seen them through, after all, so why were they so self-satisfied?

In future Christmases, after the Erector Set, the Lionel trains and the plastic Human Body with all those red and blue veins and arteries and capillaries, there would be the Rock'em, Sock'em Robots, knocking one another's heads off but coming completely assembled and requiring only battery installation, and then the General Electric record player with detachable speakers and dozens of record albums, all I ever desired besides a Dunlop Maxply tennis racket—Beatles, of course, and Stones, and the Who, and Petula Clark (we were good boys) and, later, Jethro Tull and Joe Cocker.

One year beneath our boyhood tree there were skis: Northland skis of blond wood, with bear-trap bindings, not unlike skis we had seen at Elmer Rynne's sporting goods store in Lowell a few days earlier but clearly superior as these had been fashioned at the North Pole. Our regular snow boots were sound enough to fit in the bindings, and by noon we

were out on the short hill behind our house and the Demers's, Dad hoisting us up at the bottom and carrying us back up to the top. He and Mom would drive us to ski areas for years to come, even though they didn't ski. They grew increasingly discerning about the lodges. Dad eventually deemed Loon Mountain's the best, as he had found a barman there who could make a proper martini—a drink as foreign to the ski trade as lemonade.

Kevin and I would be joined by a sister, Gail, and because of this the angled, gingerbread house in West Chelmsford would become impossibly small for the Sullivans, and would be sold to another, even younger family, and we would move into a somewhat larger, freshly built house in Chelmsford—Chelmsford proper—though the Christmases didn't change, one Christmas being so much like another in those years. Our setting changed, but our colors didn't, and Gail, too, was raised a colored-lights-and-tinsel child. She loved tinsel, and Kevin and I, eight and six when she was born and ten and eight as we gazed upon her, treeside, throwing fistfuls of tinsel onto the branches,

would reminisce: Only yesterday, I was similarly wanton, and now I am a sophisticate, hanging one silver strand at a time.

"Tinsel?" my daughter asks.

Yes, of course, my dear. Tinsel. It is—or was—a flimsy decoration, a filament of silver that would hang upon a branch and flutter in the slightest breeze. It was durable, and would be found in a corner or under the couch when cleaning the living room in July or August. Perhaps because of this, this nuisance aspect of tinsel, it went out of fashion. These days you can't find tinsel even at Target, it is so déclassé. I wonder if this saddens my adult sister, Gail. She is made of sterner stuff than I am; she is more colorful. Hers is the only tree and house in her Massachusetts neighborhood that sings with rainbow lights, rather than soft whites. Colored lights, still, and good for her—if no tinsel.

S A CHILD, Gail had an unusual attachment to "The Little Drummer Boy." She was drawn to that melody and lyric as Bernstein was moved by Mahler. Dad saw this; he noticed every little thing about his sweet girl; she was her father's daughter. One evening he returned from work with a new long-playing record. He had bought it for a dollar: actually, ninety-nine cents, a special at the gas station, a Christmas anthology that could be had for ninety-nine cents with a fill-up. He had pulled in for gas, but had left with a record when he noticed on the back of the jacket that there was a version of "The Little Drummer Boy." It could not have been by Nat Cole or Johnny Mathis or Perry Como—we already had those at home; perhaps it was by Andy Williams, or another singer who might be oft-represented on gas-station anthologies, his smiling and handsome young face framed in a red or green ornament on the cover. Dad never brought home the promotional Hess trucks—I don't think we had Hess stations in our town, and this probably would have been earlier than Hess anyway—but he brought home that album. On the Magnavox stereo that was part of the television console, we wore it out.

The new house had a better hill for sledding and perfectly rectangular rooms, and, on the day we moved in, I found myself in deep trouble for walking the two miles back to my old neighborhood to see if Paul Clancy and Mark Demers still wanted to be my friends. I remember that the trek back to West Chelmsford unfolded in chapters. I walked to the bottom of our new, longer driveway; I didn't know that I was going anywhere. I walked down Berkeley Drive; this would have been about a third of a mile. At Graniteville Road I made the dangerous decision to keep going. I took a left. I didn't know, back then, that there was a shortcut via Crooked Spring Road and a big field of unmowed grass, so I went to the intersection of Graniteville and School Street (this would all be part of my jogging route, when I was older). I went right and walked past the very old graveyard and also the abandoned white building for which this road was named long ago. Quessy School would be renovated in a few more years and would be where Kevin and I spent fifth and sixth grades, in a nineteenth-century four-room schoolhouse that was needed for four or five years to help with the flood of Baby Boomer children coming through the system. I can still smell the thick lacquer they used to get that school back to acceptability. But that day, on my adventure, I hardly noticed that building, which would be so crucial to my love of learning, as I passed. At the train tracks at Stony Brook, I stopped. Should I cross train tracks, I asked myself. I looked left, right, left again. I looked into the shack where the stationmaster sometimes sat, but it was empty on this weekend day. I looked right, left, then right. I wondered what I was doing. Then I crossed the tracks. I walked up

the hill and past the post office where Mama, Kevin and I would pick up the mail after a pleasant walk from the Main Street house; I knew I was getting close. I was careful when walking around the Dangerous Curve, which had caused our old neighborhood's only traffic accident, and then I was home free. I knocked on the Clancys' door, and Paul answered. Boy, he said, are you in trouble. My parents were in a state, apparently. Dad drove across town in the Oldsmobile and picked me up. I wasn't happy about whatever punishment I would get—it turned out to be nothing—but I was pretty happy about the adventure.

ERE MY YOUNG DAUGHTER ASKS: "Did they give you a time-out?"

We didn't have time-outs then. My parents were upset, and that was enough to make me feel bad. They never really scolded us. Kevin and I were good boys, and Gail—your aunt Gail—was a very good girl, and Mom and Dad seemed to know this.

Well, there was one night. Kevin and I were in charge of Gail, and we were rampaging around the house and one of us—Kevin or me, I can't remember—slammed one of the bedroom doors while desperately escaping from the other, and Gail's finger got caught and broken, and blood was everywhere, and I ran down the street to Dr. Archambault's house, and that night Dad took off his belt and threatened to use it on Kevin and me. But he didn't. Even then, he didn't. I think he saw that we were scared enough. Even as he brandished the belt, I knew he wouldn't use it. Something told me that he couldn't. He stood there for a long moment, thinking, and then left and shut the door. Aunt Gail's finger is still crooked.

She says, "Get back to Christmas."

Yes, Christmas.

UR TREE could be a bit bigger in the new house, as the main room was larger, and we began to decorate outdoors as well as inside. Nothing ostentatious, but a few lights around the front door and on the wrought-iron railings. A Christmas or two went by, and then we kids started to protest with Dad that we should build a fire in the fireplace at Christmastime. But he said no. We hadn't built one since moving in, and he was convinced that squirrels and birds had built nests of dry-as-bones, highly inflammable materials in the chimney. He was scared to death of another house fire. We didn't argue. As it was, this probably made it easier for Santa, anyway. And we were warm enough.

One Christmas or another, we were given sleds. Flexible Flyers. We used them so early and often that the fancy red paint on their runners was worn off within a week of Christmas Day. In our new neighborhood, we could stretch the playing field, as they now say during the football games. When the proper confluence of snow and wind and rain and depth-of-base and quality of top-dressing occurred, we could start at the Strojnys' backyard (two houses north), proceed through the Dahlgrens' flat, zoom onto the Sullivan Slope and then . . .

Usually, the ride ended there, as we spun out. But in extraordinary circumstances, it extended. One cold day we brought buckets of water to the street and built an ice bridge across the Berkeley Drive asphalt that had already been plowed by the town. This allowed our racecourse to enter the Reeds' yard, then the Moseleys', and then hop onto the recently cut Windsor Place, which was to be part of a new housing development but at the time was just a downhill dirt avenue—covered in snow—that descended all the way to the stream. The full route was nearly half a mile long, though I see it as equal to the

Boston Marathon. We would compete belly-down on our sleds, one boy stationed at the Berkeley Drive Crossing to instruct us to bail out if the rare car was coming. We vied ferociously, teeth clenched and eyes ablaze in the cold. If you were gaining on the boy just ahead and could grab his rear runner and spin him off the course, well, of course you would do so. I was a heavy boy—Husky, in my Mighty Mac winter coat—and would often gain speed during a race, nipping up on those who had started with more nimbleness and alacrity. I would do my damage, leaving wreckage in my wake. I did not cackle; I wasn't that kind of kid. I stayed within myself, smiling only inside, enjoying the thrill of the race, my fingers numb beyond pain (that would come with the thawing), as alive as alive can be. I was an afternoon-into-evening sledder; I remember many a darkening dusk climbing back toward the yellow warmth of home. I remember, too, one triumphant race when I was truly flying. I beat all comers and jumped the snowbank at the bottom of Windsor Place. I wound up splayed on the barbed wire that ran alongside the stream. My pillowed parka was punctured and ripped as I extricated myself; I bled near both wrists; perhaps I had cut the crucial artery. I picked up my sled and started to trudge uphill, very happily thinking three things: I'm not irrevocably broken, How much trouble am I in, and, *What a run.*

"Did you have a Christmas puppy?" my daughter asks inevitably. "Did she chase you on the sled?"

No, but there was a dog. A dog named Duchess. And before her one named Peppy. Neither was a Christmas dog—or, as you say, a Christmas puppy—but both fell out of the sky as if Santa brought them for us. One stayed a little while, and the other forever.

"Which was first?"

Peppy was first.

OTH WERE MUTTS whose owners wanted to be rid of them. Dogs roamed free in Chelmsford then, and they met one another, fell in love and made babies—sometimes right in the street. Peppy happened at a house down Berkeley Drive where a golden retriever lived, and these people asked Mom at a cocktail party if we wanted one of the puppies that was imminently due, and Mom probably said, "Oh, sure," and then that family went on vacation and the Littles, a family just across the street and up two houses, called and said, "Your new dog is in our garage. The So-and-sos left it with us before they went away."

This was Peppy, a black, vivacious dog who grew to be huge. Her strong and sweeping tail was precisely even with the top of the coffee table that fronted our paisley couch, and before letting Peppy in at the porch door, we had to clear away all glasses and plates, lest they be swept to smithereens. Peppy stayed a little while. She was energetic, as I say, and one of the local kids, a little boy named David, claimed Peppy had bitten him. Peppy hadn't, but David's parents made a stink—and this was well before parents made a stink about every little thing. These people kept up the stink, they just wouldn't let it be, and finally Dad and Mom had to send Peppy away to A Farm in Vermont.

"What about Duchess?"

She stayed forever. Duchess grew up with us.

I had a paper route. My friend Mike, two years older, handed down to me his *Boston Globe* paper route, and Kevin and I split the workload and eventually grew the enterprise to forty or fifty, perhaps even sixty houses. We would rise at five thirty most of the year, six thirty in summer, and head out on our bikes. I enjoyed delivering the papers each morning, although I didn't much enjoy collecting the seventy-seven cents from people on Friday afternoons. (God bless those who tipped twenty-three cents; not all did.) After I parked my bike, kickstand down, and walked to the door of each house, I would read parts of articles; I think I got my political

persuasion from the *Globe*, and I greatly enjoyed Bud Collins and Ray Fitzgerald in the sports pages (I thought Clif Keane was mean). I looked forward to delivering papers in winter as well as summer—winter, when sometimes the snow was deep enough and the roads so slippery that Kevin and I had to walk, not bike, the route, laboring under bulging canvas *Boston Globe* carrying bags slung over our shoulders. In December, occasionally, the weather and the onrushing holiday would conspire to make affairs difficult: The newspapers would grow fat with Christmas advertising as the temperature dropped, the wind rose up and the snow started to fly. Still, I didn't mind. It was a good way to wake up each day. And I was eager. Christmas was coming.

"What about Duchess?"

Oh, yes, of course. She came with the paper route. I was about to talk about Duchess. She made me think of the paper route.

She followed me home one day; she was no bigger than a loaf of bread, nipping along at my heels as I pedaled. She wanted to play. I knew where she was from immediately. The house right at the curve of the horseshoe on Charlemont Court had, just a week previous, been blessed with a litter of puppies. This was one.

Certainly I encouraged her. I was a boy with a bike on a Saturday and this was an infant puppy with an abundance of spunk. Here, girl!

Kevin, returning from his half of the route, was of course thrilled with my find. We brought the yet-unnamed Duchess upstairs and into Dad and Mom's room, where they were just awakening. The puppy scampered around on their bed for a short time and everyone was amused. But Dad was adamant. He said: "A dog as fine as this belongs to someone. You have to find out whom."

Duchess, now named, slept downstairs that night, where she peed on the *Globe*, and the next morning I dutifully led her back out on the paper route. I even knocked on the door of the family where Duchess had been born.

"My father wants me to ask if this dog is yours," I said. "She followed me home."

The woman was horror-struck: "I've never seen that dog!" She was tempted to slam the door, but wouldn't do so in the face of a child, and so she closed it firmly. And quickly. She wasn't a subscriber, and wasn't about to wait for me to hand her the fat Sunday paper.

Duchess stayed eighteen years. She claimed a chair in the living room as her own, and since she did this sheepishly at first, Dad proclaimed that, clearly: "She is well bred." She wandered the neighborhood, the woods and even the greater town, and made many friends. Twice, people tried to steal her. One time, I took her away from two other boys who were leading her by the collar down Graniteville Road. I saw this happening, up ahead: two boys, one bent over with his hand in the collar of my own dog. I was terrified but felt that I needed to confront them. Shaking, I said, "That's my dog!" The boys were my age. They looked at me and let go of Duchess. They never said a word. Duchess and I walked home. I didn't stop shaking for an hour.

A second time, Duchess was gone for four days and when she returned wearing a new collar, Mom, who liked Duchess well enough but hadn't, until now, been a Duchess defender, went to war. She bought a newer-still collar at J. M. Fields, threw the kidnappers' collar in the trash, and made sure our dog stayed close to home until the old rhythms had returned. She was weaning Duchess off the kidnappers' kindnesses. Mom eventually found out who the kidnappers were, and that their young daughters had probably put them up to it, and maybe because of that she didn't make an issue.

In later years, Duchess ran up against what was called, in the new Chelmsford and everywhere else, a leash law. We couldn't leash her—we simply couldn't, not at her age—and so we paid the fine whenever she was happy enough to jump into the dog officer's van. She did this often enough; she liked the dog officer. He might even have had treats. One day, I saw the dog officer, parked in front of the Moseleys' house, beckoning to her while she dozed on our front lawn. I came down the front steps and said, "Hey, that's unfair! She lives here!" The dog officer, upbraided by a twelve-year-old, drove off, his quota unmet.

Duchess continued to wander. Many of us hung out our laundry to dry in those days, even into December, and I remember once seeing Duchess happily trotting up the street with a bra in her mouth, one cup bouncing off each jowl. We determined this was the bra of the exotically named Mina Holland, who lived three houses down, though Mina never was bold enough to reclaim it. It wasn't necessarily a Christmas bra, but it was red, and that Mina Holland had let it blow in the breeze in the first place remains an astonishment.

Duchess, the pleasantest mutt you've ever known, spent dinnertime with us each night, reclining—if alertly—beneath the kitchen table. Dad would cut off a piece of steak and then would, he thought surreptitiously, hand it down. "Artie," Mom would say. "Do you know what that costs at DeMoulas?"

"Oh, Lucille," Dad would say. "Duchess isn't going to be with us that much longer." Duchess was six when I first witnessed this, and, as I say, she stayed with us, steak-fed and happy, until age eighteen.

"Did you feed her steak only at Christmas?" my daughter asks.

We always fed her steak and other treats at Christmas. But Dad fed her steak whenever we had it.

"Was steak your Christmas dinner?"

No, it wasn't. Turkey was. We were one of those families that had turkey at Thanksgiving, and another turkey at Christmas. I'm not sure why. Maybe because it took all night to cook, and therefore seemed special. Whatever meant more work was better.

URKEY WAS PART OF OUR CHRISTMAS, as was the tree with bubblers, as was the trip to the Bon Marché Santa in Lowell and the Enchanted Village at Jordan Marsh in Boston. The Enchanted Village was small: replica towns and buildings, something like the vastest and most glowing Lionel railroad landscape you've ever seen.

"We went to the Enchanted Village last year," my daughter says correctly. "Remember? When we visited Aunt Gail and Uncle Scott and Callie and Jamie? We went to the Enchanted Village."

Well, yes, we did. But it . . . It changed at some point, and the figures of people became life-sized, the buildings became painted backdrops. That's what you saw last year.

When Kevin and I and young Gail went to the Enchanted Village at Jordan Marsh, everything was very small. I wondered what was going on in each of those tiny houses. Gail and Kevin and I peered in, and we exchanged our guesses. What were they doing to prepare for Christmas. Were they as excited as we were. Of course they were. Turkey. Maybe. Or roast beef. I think the Dahlgren family had roast beef.

And then we would go from Jordan Marsh to Bailey's, and enjoy sundaes in pewter cups, even on the coldest of December days, with the hot fudge and marshmallow cascading over the edge into the pewter catch-basin plates. Years later, *The Nutcracker* and even *The Messiah* would be special. But not yet—not hardly.

"Were there parties?"

HERE ARE ALWAYS PARTIES at Christmas. Parties or, at least, get-togethers.

My parents would open our doors to a few of Dad's colleagues shortly before Christmas, and Norbert Parent and his wife would come, as would Ray Hathawate and his wife. They would sit and smoke and have a few drinks, and the Parents would leave us with a gift-wrapped bottle of Chivas Regal, as would the Hathawates. Dad, as I said, was a martini drinker, but appreciated the gesture that Chivas represented. I enjoyed, from afar, the company of the modest Parents and Hathawates; they affirmed for me my faith in my father. Good company. No one left drunk.

Later there were Christmas Eve parties, Mom returning to her heritage and putting out rich food, fish as the centerpiece, as had all the French in Lowell for generations—and the Italians in Gloucester and Lawrence—as had they all, for generations. If there was smoked cod, the baccalà, in Gloucester, on Mom's table there was fondue and coquilles Saint-Jacques and, my favorite, lobster Newburg, which I would address with both a fork and a spoon. These parties burgeoned as I grew older, becoming almost raucous—too much so for Dad. Mom and her Newburg grew to be famous among my high school friends. Several years on, I and Mike and Barry and Bruce would walk with any overage of food up the street and then down Old Westford Road to the firemen who were working

through the night at the Roberts Field firehouse. It is interesting to me how fire departments keep coming up: the burning house, the hand grenades, now this. Maybe, now, with my high school friends, I was saying thank you for the firemen of West Chelmsford, years earlier. I remember that the firemen of the Roberts Field station were happy to see us, even though they surely realized that here were four teenage boys who had had a bit of wine. The grateful firemen enjoyed the food we brought, and gave us a tour of the trucks.

My daughter says: "Mama made a party on Christmas Eve last year, too." My children call my mother Mama, just as I called my mother's mother Mama.

Yes, I say to her: It's the same party. These days, Mom's parties are back to family again, and that firehouse is fully automated, triggered to spring into action and summon the firemen the moment a computer tells it to do so. There are no men or women on duty Christmas Eve. Not anymore.

And yes, there have always been parties, and there continue to be parties, and when I was a boy—just like today—there was a feast. The processional of the day has never varied. I can say that much. One Christmas was always the same as the other, and it still is, which is good.

We would rise excitedly, we would rip open the presents, we would present to our parents meager gifts (a cheap wallet or a tie tack; a paste necklace or a brooch), we would run outside and try the outside toys in the snow. It always snowed at Christmas back then.

"It still snows for Christmas."

Not like it snowed back then. Kevin and I would take our shovels to the driveway on Christmas morning, and make certain the way was clear for Mama and Aunt Margot. There was always so much snow, piles of snow. That was part of the day's processional, too: the shoveling.

And the presents, and the play, and then the stamping of feet as Mom began to put out the feast. Dad would open the oysters with a screwdriver, and we would start with those—an acquired taste that I would not acquire for quite a number of years. During the hors d'oeuvres hour I would eat the small hot dogs or would coat a piece

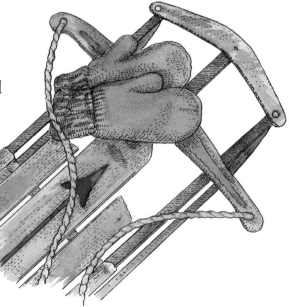

of bread with cheese fondue. Both of these epicurean exercises entailed the use of toothpicks, and my collection of expended toothpicks would grow to a dozen, a score, and more. Mom always used multicolored plastic toothpicks at Christmas.

HEN WE WOULD SIT FOR DINNER, which was the precise same dinner we had sat for a month earlier: turkey and stuffing and cranberries and potatoes drenched in butter and creamed onions and brussels sprouts, the only vegetable I could abide besides corn on the cob, which was not available in December. This dinner signaled a special occasion, and would only be featured on these two most special of days, when family gathered.

"You said there was an aunt?"

An aunt, and a grandmother.

They lived together in Lowell, in that large house I mentioned, the one in which my mother had been born—a widow, my grandmother, and the aunt, who was what was called an old maid. Mama, the grandmother I have spoken of, was tiny and friendly and I always thought she was smart. She would babysit us when Mom went to work or when, once a year, Dad and Mom went to the racetrack at Rockingham Park in New Hampshire, placing, in addition to their own wagers, one two-dollar bet for Mama on whatever horse sounded, in name, most French. Ooh-la-la would do fine, or Mais Oui. The French horses never came through. Dad and Mom's deal with Mama—and with us—was that, if they made money, they would be home an hour and a half later than planned, as they would stop at Valle's Steak House for shared châteaubriand, whereas if they lost they would forgo the romantic late-afternoon splurge. Mama babysat us on these occasions and many others until one day, in the large kitchen of the large house on Mount Vernon Street, the popcorn started sailing all over the place, which delighted me and Kevin, but worried Mom when she walked in and found her own mother confused and sad. The senility, as it was called, would progress to include a car accident and another near thing with Mama's own Mercury, and then, one Christmas, an incontinent episode when I was sitting alongside Mama at the family dinner table. I might have been twelve or thirteen. It was one of the first times in my life I felt proud of myself. I let Mom know what had happened, discreetly, and it was taken care of without comment and then the meal continued.

Another of those times of pride involved the aunt, Margot, who as I say was Mama's sister. Margot lived her life as an appendage to Mama, until Mama died. Margot then moved out of the Mount Vernon Street house—it was impossible for her after Mama died, impossibly big and impossibly poignant—and into a small apartment around the block. As I grew a bit older, I saw her precisely once a year, on Christmas Day. One year, the storm was enormous. Dad and Mom speculated that Margot might not be able to share dinner with us (she had never had a driver's license; we would fetch her each year). Dad was putting the screwdriver to the oysters as he said, "It's getting pretty bad."

"I'll go get her," I said. I was bigger now.

Mom and Dad were okay with this. I drove the Oldsmobile Cutlass to Margot's snow-filled block, a Lowell side street, and pressed the button for her apartment. She let me in. She was sitting in a chair in front of a picture of the Virgin Mary. It is hard to impress upon another person just how diminutive Margot was. When Mama had still been alive, Margot made tiny Mama look like a big person—an impossibility. Here she was, small and frail, and cognizant of the storm. I'm not sure we even said hello to each other. She began to cry as she took my arm. Back in Chelmsford, we had a fine meal, and I or Dad or Kevin drove her home afterward.

"What did you do after dinner?"

After dinner?

Well, that year, I remember, I thought about Margot, back in her apartment. I wondered if she still had the souvenirs we had bought for her at the monastery when we were younger. I was in bed, looking at the ceiling. I said some words to the close and holy darkness, and then I slept.

ROBERT SULLIVAN, collaborator with Glenn Wolff on *Flight of the Reindeer* and *Atlantis Rising* and author of several other books, is the Managing Editor of LIFE Books. That's him on the left in his Mighty Mac parka, posing with his brother Kevin and a fellow named Claus sometime in the late 1950s. Sullivan has since married and fathered children of his own—three of them—and lives with his family and their nutty Springer Spaniel in Westchester County, New York.

GLENN WOLFF, pictured here in the early 1960s between brother Paul, sister Lisa, and their short-wheelbase Golden Retriever named Gomer, lives and works in Northern Michigan. Over the years his own children have appreciated a rich holiday tapestry that includes both Christmas trees and menorahs. In addition to illuminating the worlds of real and mythical creatures for Robert Sullivan and numerous other authors including Jerry Dennis, John Gierach and Janine Benyus, Glenn has contributed illustrations for more than thirty years to *The New York Times*.